THIS WALKER BOOK BELONGS TO:

_____

_____

_____

For Will and Nat, who like toys
H.C.

First published 1999 by Walker Books Ltd
87 Vauxhall Walk, London SE11 5HJ

This edition published 2004

2 4 6 8 10 9 7 5 3 1

Text © 1999 Joyce Dunbar
Illustrations © 1999 Helen Craig Ltd

The right of Joyce Dunbar and Helen Craig to be identified
as author and illustrator respectively of this work has been
asserted by them in accordance with the Copyright,
Designs and Patents Act 1988

This book has been typeset in Alpha Normal

Printed in China

British Library Cataloguing in Publication Data:
a catalogue record for this book is
available from the British Library

ISBN 0-7445-6387-9

www.walkerbooks.co.uk

PaNDa and Gander

Panda's New Toy

Joyce Dunbar illustrated by Helen Craig

WALKER BOOKS
AND SUBSIDIARIES
LONDON · BOSTON · SYDNEY · AUCKLAND

Panda had a new toy.
It was a cup and a ball.
The ball was fastened to
the cup with a piece
of string.

"How do you play with it?"
asked Gander.

"The game is to swing the ball and
catch it in the cup," said Panda.

"I'll show you."

Panda swung the ball and ...

missed.

He swung it again and ...

missed again!

He swung it and missed,

again ...

and again.

5

"Will you let me try now?" asked Gander.

"Wait until I've got it right,"
said Panda.

Panda swung
the ball again ...
and caught it!

"See, Gander. I caught the ball in the cup.
That's what you have to do."

"Just watch."
Panda swung the ball ...
and missed!

But then he swung it and caught it,
again ...

and again.

"Now will you let me try?" asked Gander.
"It might be too difficult for you,"
said Panda.

"It looks easy," said Gander.
"It's easy for me," said Panda. "So easy
I think I could catch it with my eyes
closed. Let's see."

Panda swung the ball and caught it
with his eyes closed.

"Is it my turn now?" asked Gander.
"I think I could even catch it
standing on one leg," said Panda
"Watch this."

So Panda swung the ball and caught it
standing on one leg.

"That's clever," said Gander.

"Is it my turn now?"

"I want to see if I can eat a biscuit with
one paw and catch the ball with the other,"
said Panda.

Panda ate a biscuit with one paw and caught the ball with the other.

"Now it's my turn," said Gander.
"First I want to see if I can swing on the swing and still catch the ball in the cup," said Panda.

So Gander pushed Panda on the swing
while Panda caught the ball in the cup.
"I think I could be an acrobat," said Panda.

"I think you could," said Gander,

"but it's my turn now."

"I'll just have one last turn," said Panda.

"You've had lots of last turns," said Gander.

"A really last turn," said Panda.

So Panda had a really last turn.

But he swung the ball too hard
and broke the string!
Away rolled the ball.

Gander went running to fetch it.

"Now I won't be able to have a turn,"
said Gander.

"Yes, you will," said Panda.

And he tied a knot in the string so that
the ball was fastened to the cup again.

"Good," said Gander. "Now can I have a go?"

"Let me see if it works first," said Panda.

"The string might be too long or too short."

"Panda," said Gander.

"What is it?" said Panda.

"I don't care if the string is
   too long or too short.

I don't want to play with that toy
any more. I'm going to play with
the jolly trolley."
"Gander," said
Panda.

"What is it?" said Gander.
"It's your turn with the cup and
the ball. I want to play with the
jolly trolley."

"Good," said Gander to Panda, "because it's my turn for a ride on the jolly trolley and your turn to pull it along."

And riding along on the jolly trolley,
Gander swung the ball in the cup and –
caught it!

WALKER BOOKS is the world's leading
independent publisher of children's books.
Working with the best authors and illustrators
we create books for all ages, from babies
to teenagers – books your child will
grow up with and always remember. So…

FOR THE BEST CHILDREN'S BOOKS,
LOOK FOR THE BEAR